TIME FOR SCHOOL, BABY SHARK

Doo Doo Doo Doo Doo Doo

Art by John John Bajet

SCHOLASTIC

This edition published in the UK in 2020 by Scholastic Children's Books
Euston House, 24 Eversholt Street, London NW1 1DB
A division of Scholastic Ltd
www.scholastic.co.uk
London – New York – Toronto – Sydney – Auckland – Mexico City – New Delhi – Hong Kong

First published in 2020 by Cartwheel Books, an imprint of Scholastic Inc., U.S.A.
Copyright © Scholastic Inc., 2020
Adapted from the song, "Baby Shark".

ISBN 978 0702 30527 6

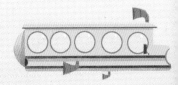

The first day is here,
And all through the ocean
The creatures are buzzing
With school-day commotion.

Come on, **BABY SHARK**!
There's nothing to fear.
Time to get ready.
The bus is almost here!

Let's get dressed, doo doo doo doo doo doo.
Let's get dressed, doo doo doo doo doo doo.

Let's get dressed, doo doo doo doo doo doo.
LET'S GET DRESSED!

Backpack on, doo doo doo doo doo doo.
Backpack on, doo doo doo doo doo doo.

Backpack on, doo doo doo doo doo doo.
BACKPACK ON!

Board the bus, doo doo doo doo doo doo.
Board the bus, doo doo doo doo doo doo.

SCHOOL OF FISH

Board the bus, doo doo doo doo doo doo doo.

BOARD THE BUS!

Say hello, doo doo doo doo doo doo.
Say hello, doo doo doo doo doo doo.

Say hello, doo doo doo doo doo doo.
SAY HELLO!

WELCOME, CLASS!

Find your space, doo doo doo doo doo doo.
Find your space, doo doo doo doo doo doo.

Find your space, doo doo doo doo doo doo.

FIND YOUR SPACE!

Story time, doo doo doo doo doo doo doo.
Story time, doo doo doo doo doo doo doo.

Once upon a time . . .

Story time, doo doo doo doo doo doo.

STORY TIME!

Sing a song, doo doo doo doo doo doo.
Sing a song, doo doo doo doo doo doo doo.

Sing a song, doo doo doo doo doo doo.
SING A SONG!

Make a friend, doo doo doo doo doo doo.
Make a friend, doo doo doo doo doo doo.

Make a friend, doo doo doo doo doo doo.

MAKE A FRIEND!

Share your snack, doo doo doo doo doo doo.
Share your snack, doo doo doo doo doo doo doo.

SHARE YOUR SNACK!

Play all day, doo doo doo doo doo doo doo.
Play all day, doo doo doo doo doo doo doo.
Play all day, doo doo doo doo doo doo doo.

PLAY ALL DAY!

HAVE FUN AT SCHOOL,
BABY SHARK!

TIME FOR SCHOOL, BABY SHARK DANCE!

LET'S GET DRESSED!

Put on an imaginary jacket one sleeve at a time.

BACKPACK ON!

Secure your backpack straps.

BOARD THE BUS!

Step in place.

SAY HELLO!

Wave hello.

FIND YOUR SPACE!

Put your hand over your eyes and search.

STORY TIME!

Sit down and open your hands like a book.

SING A SONG!

Sing a song and bob your head back and forth.

MAKE A FRIEND!

Pretend to lock arms with your new friend.

SHARE YOUR SNACK!

Put your hand out.

PLAY ALL DAY!

Act crazy!